Leap's Day

By
Stephanie Bee Simmons

AuthorHouse™
1663 Liberty Drive
Bloomington, IN 47403
www.authorhouse.com
Phone: 1-800-839-8640

First published by AuthorHouse 11/29/2011

ISBN: 978-1-4685-0739-3 (sc)

Library of Congress Control Number: 201196150220

Printed in the United States of America

Any people depicted in stock imagery provided by Thinkstock are models,
and such images are being used for illustrative purposes only.
Certain stock imagery © Thinkstock.

authorHOUSE®

For Andrew

Born February 29, 2000
I Love You!

Kersplash! Leap quickly hurried off,
He headed toward the land.
Leap rushed to find his father,
To share what he had planned.

Leap swam as fast as he could go,
From rock to rock he hopped.
When at last he found his dad,
Leap skidded to a stop.

Son, you're so excited.
Stop jumping all around.
Tell me what is on your mind.
Take a breath! Slow down!

I was resting on my lily pad,
Watching my friends at play.
When I realized each was special,
In a different sort of way.

Ray is always patient,
Mary Lou knows how to listen,
Stu's always there to lend a hand,
The kindest one is Kristen.

I think it would be grand if they
Each had a special date.
Perhaps the day that they were born
We all could celebrate.

So Dad, will you please help me,
Use the lines upon this wall?
You never let a day slip by,
You keep track of them all.

Most all the lines are drawn in black,
There's yellow in between,
But on a day a frog is born,
The line is always green.

But Leap, the lines mean nothing.
They just track the days gone by.
But if it's that important,
We'll sure give it a try.

We know that we get older,
Just look at Grandpa Pete.
So in a certain span of time,
The days must all repeat.

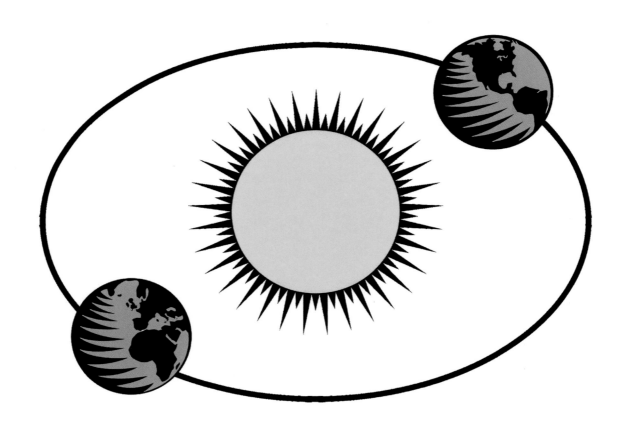

Let's take the days and sort them out,
We'll make some smaller sets.
Let's think about the Earth and sun,
And see what we can get.

Earth makes a path around the sun,
That could be our first group.
It takes three hundred and sixty-five days,
For Earth to make the loop.

Leap jumped up and he shouted.
He danced and gave a cheer.
I know, I know, I know, I know,
Let's call that group a "YEAR".

$$31 + 28 + 31 + 30 + 31 + 30 + 31 + 31 + 30 + 31 + 30 + 31 = 365$$

Gee, that's so much better,
Than what we had before.
Let's add another group called "MONTH",
And break it down some more.

We'll give some months just 30 days,
But most months 31.
Let's give one only 28,
Oh, that will make it fun!

"The calendar is finished!"
Leap's dad said with a smile.
Before we share it with your friends,
Let's watch it for a while.

I know the nighttime sky is dark,
And in the day it's bright.
What other clues will tell us,
That we got it all just right?

The weather changes gradually,
As the Earth goes 'round the sun.
And when day one is back again,
We'll know the year is done.

11

Watching days and months go by
For a year or so,
The problem was quite small at first,
But then began to grow.

Days that once were cold
Had suddenly turned hot.
And days that once were warm
Now suddenly were not.

Leap, we need to fix it!
This year will never do!
I think we need another day,
Or maybe even two.

"Oh, no!" they cried and shook their heads.
The extra day's too much!
But you can't split a day apart
Like pizza pies and such.

"I've got it, Dad." Leap shouted,
This will work for sure.
Don't add a day every year,
Just add one every four!

Awesome, Leap! That's super!
Your plan sounds really fine.
Let's pick the month that's shortest,
And add day 29!

Be careful where you put it, Dad.
This is a special date.
Remember there are three years first,
With just day 28!

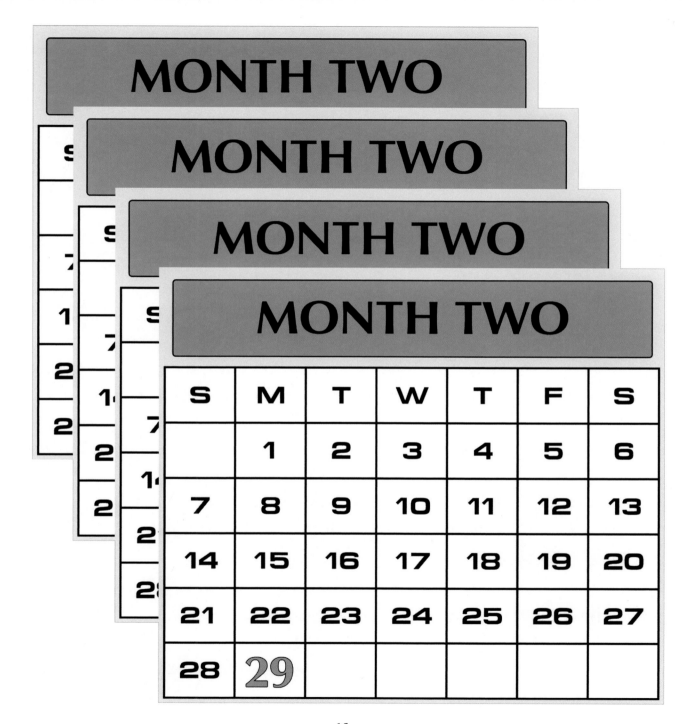

MONTH TWO

MONTH TWO

MONTH TWO

MONTH TWO

S	M	T	W	T	F	S
	1	2	3	4	5	6
7	8	9	10	11	12	13
14	15	16	17	18	19	20
21	22	23	24	25	26	27
28	29					

January

December

February

November

March

October

April

May

September

June

August

July

It's still a number mish-mosh
Let's give each month a name.
With a name and number,
No date will be the same.

January will start us off,
December can be the last.
Ten more months are in between
The years fly by so fast.

It's perfect now, I'm certain.
I can't wait to know just when
Will be that special day
For each one of my friends.

Working very carefully,
They matched the squares to lines.
They quickly figured out the dates
That they were trying to find.

Ray was born on April 1st,
Mary Lou the 3rd of May.
Stu arrived September 12th,
June 8th is Kristen's day.

Just then Leap's dad exclaimed,
"Jeepers, could this be true?
Leap, of all the calendar days,
We matched this one to you!"

February 29th!
Dad, don't look so sad.
It's the finest birthday
That I could ever have.

But Leap, have you forgotten,
There are years without that date?
Let's look again – let's double check,
There must be some mistake!

But when they checked it out again,
The result remained the same.
The special day that made it work,
Was where they placed Leap's name.

Dad, it's going to be alright,
I love the day that's mine.
And when he looked up at his son,
There was a twinkle in his eye.

Leap, you're right, you've made me proud,
It couldn't be more true.
In fact, that very special day
I think we'll name for you.

Made in the USA
Middletown, DE
08 February 2020

84346539R00018